D0461119

ONCE I WAS...

Niki Clark Leopold

ILLUSTRATED BY

Woodleigh Marx Hubbard

G. P. PUTNAM'S SONS

Once I was an alphabet,

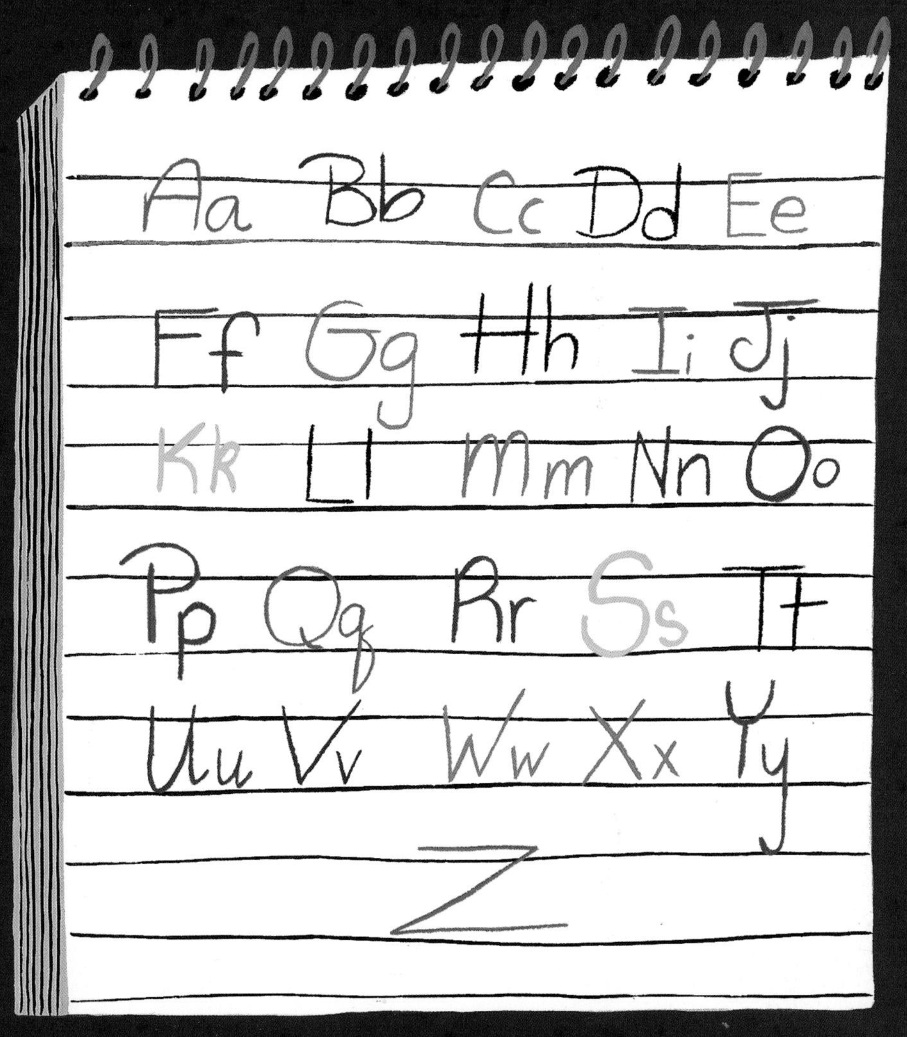

now I am a book.

Once I couldn't feed myself,

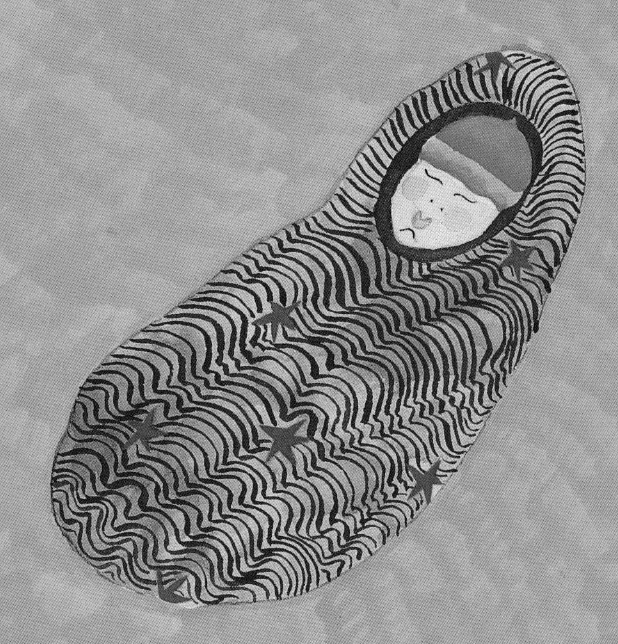

now I love to cook.

I used to be a penny,
now I am the sun.

Once I couldn't even walk,

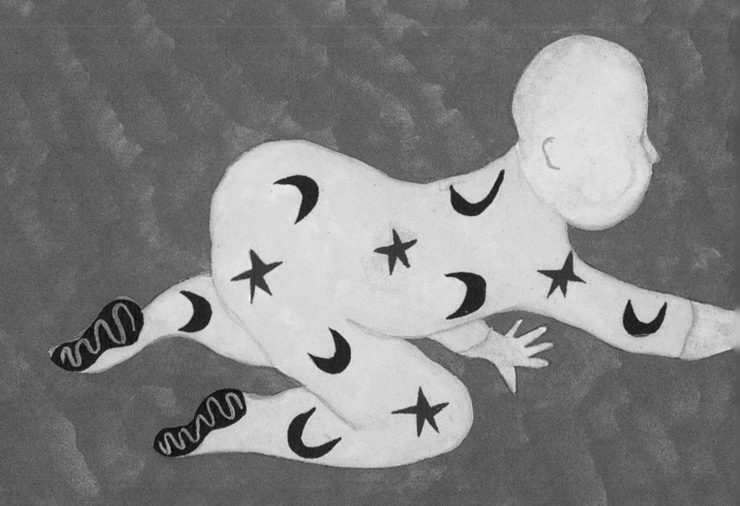

now I always run.

I used to be afraid to swim,

now I am a mermaid.

Once I couldn't comb my hair,

now I make a braid.

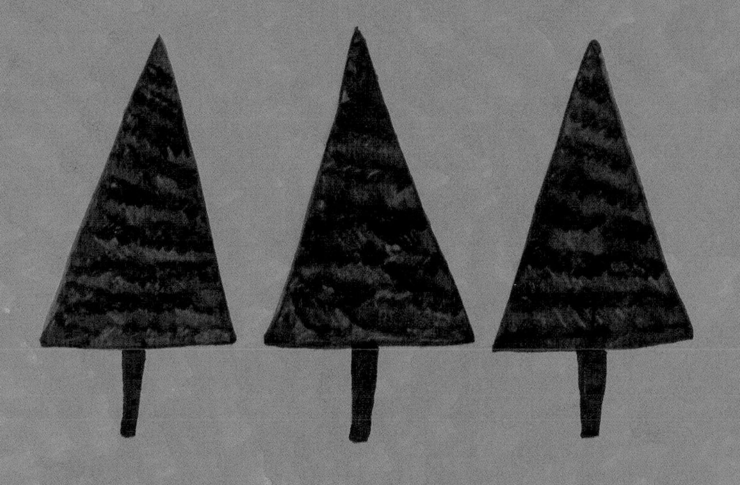

I used to be a pine cone,
now I am a forest.

Once I sang alone,

now I am a chorus.

Once I was a trickle,

now I am a lake.

I used to be the recipe,

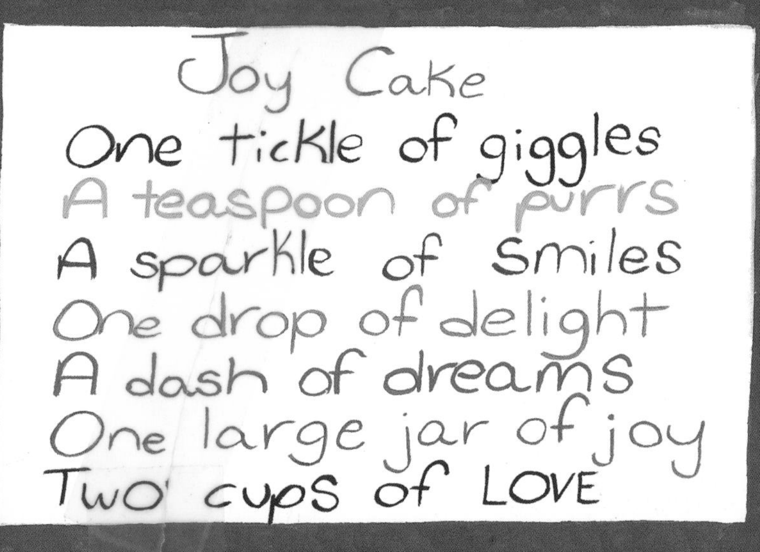
Joy Cake
One tickle of giggles
A teaspoon of purrs
A sparkle of smiles
One drop of delight
A dash of dreams
One large jar of joy
Two cups of LOVE

now I am the cake.

I used to be a napkin,
now I am a kite.

Once the dark was scary,

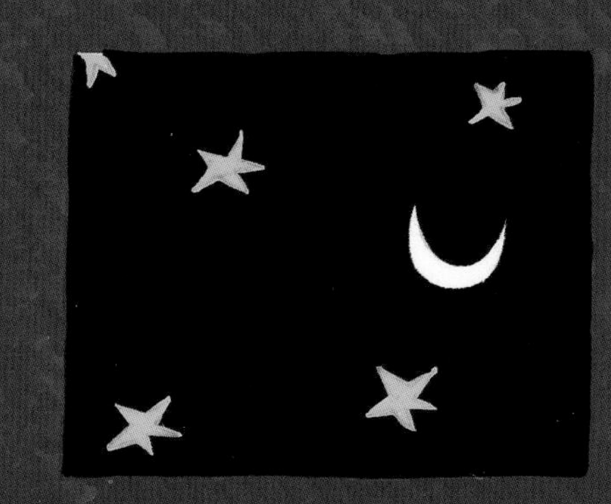

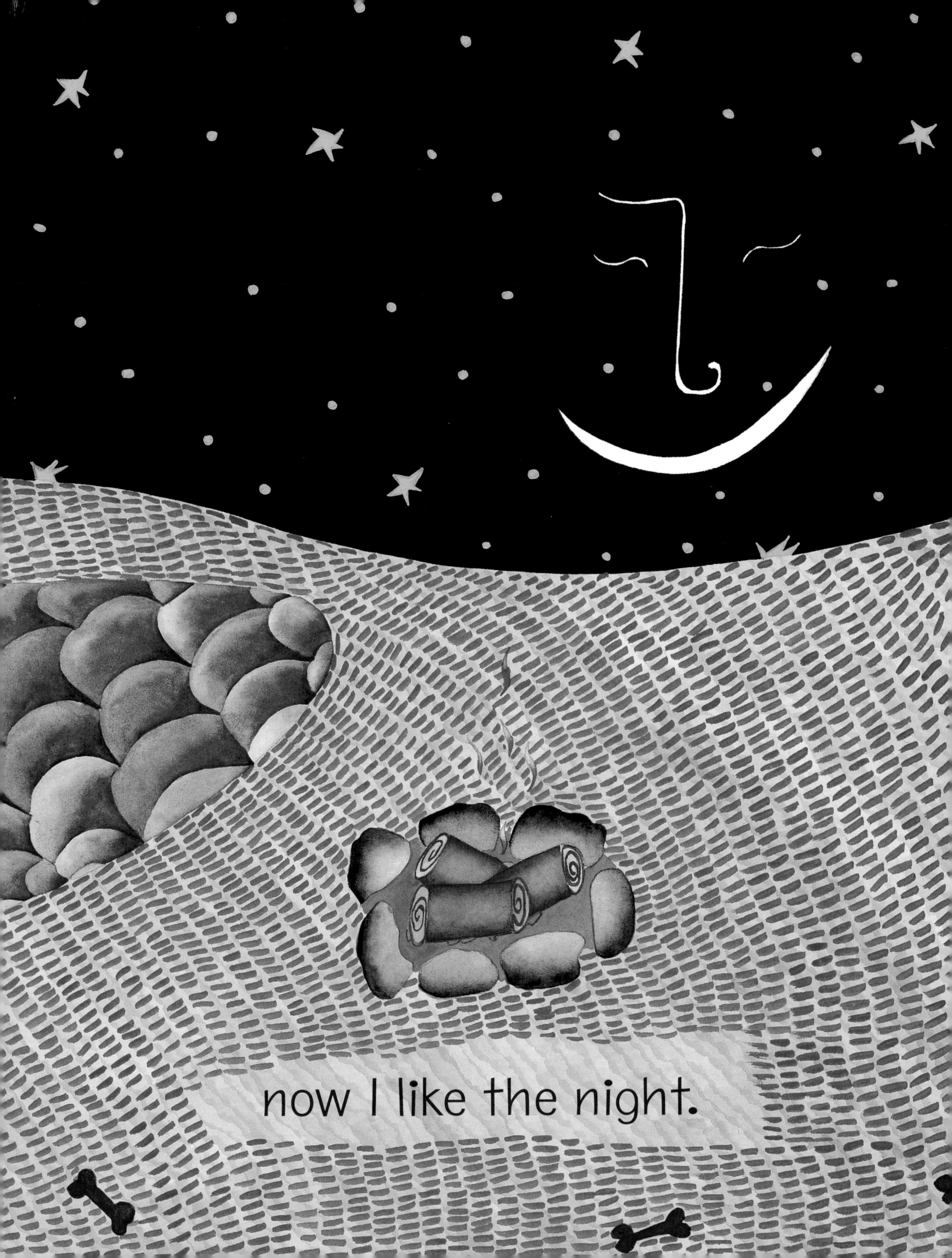

now I like the night.

Once I was a ball of yarn,

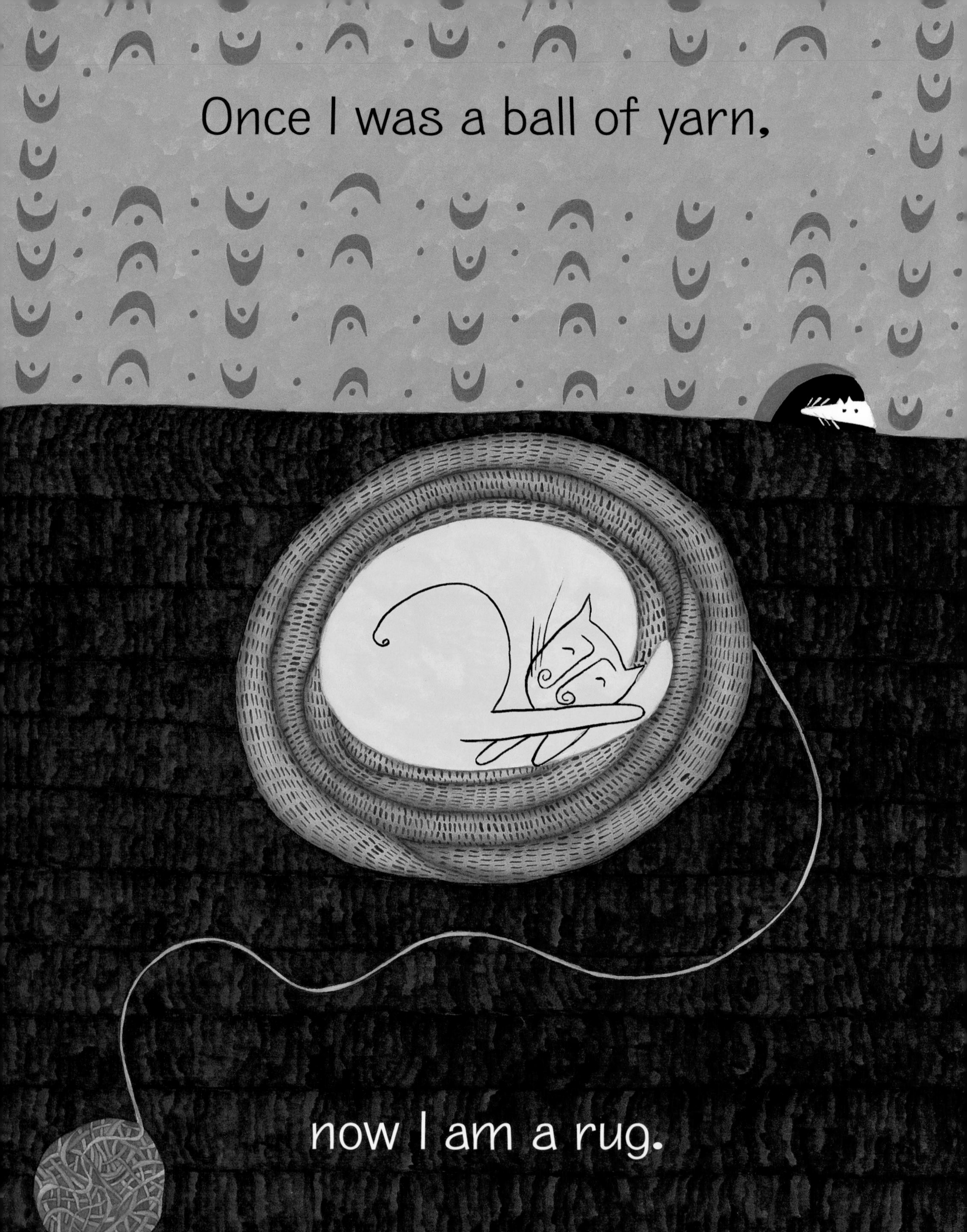

now I am a rug.

I used to be a handshake.

now I am a hug.

Once I was a whisper,

now I am the wind.

I used to play alone.

but now I have

a friend.

For Bruce, once, now and always

—N. C. L.

For Dr. Jerry J. Mallett, Claire Barnett and Niki Leopold for the inspiration, support and friendship you bring to my life.

—W. M. H.

Gratitude to Nancy Paulsen, Cecilia Yung, Donna Mark and Andrea Brown for being such a pleasure to work with on this book.

—W. M. H.

 G. P. Putnam's Sons, a division of Penguin Putnam Books for Young Readers, 345 Hudson Street, New York, NY 10014.
G. P. Putnam's Sons, Reg. U.S. Pat. & Tm. Off. Published simultaneously in Canada.
Printed in Hong Kong by South China Printing Co. (1988) Ltd. Designed by Donna Mark.
Text set in Birdlegs. Library of Congress Cataloging-in-Publication Data
Leopold, Niki Clark. Once I was... / by Niki Clark Leopold;
illustrated by Woodleigh Marx Hubbard. p. cm. Summary: A rhyming expression of the exciting growth and change experienced in childhood. [1. Growth—Fiction. 2. Stories in rhyme.] I. Hubbard, Woodleigh, ill. II. Title. PZ8.3.L549270n 1999
[E]—dc21 98-15461 CIP AC ISBN 0-399-23105-6
1 3 5 7 9 10 8 6 4 2
First Impression